T5-DHI-792

Hello,

I'm Crocus, the magician gnome. For hundreds of years we gnomes have lived high up in the forest, cut off from the folk who live in the woods.

A terrible flood brought us together a while ago and since then we have had many lively adventures.

Join us and read about, Tortoise who is learning to ride a scooter, how we take a trip in a hot-air balloon, with disastrous results, how we make a submarine to recover the Golden Key at the bottom of the pond, and how we rescue the gnomes lost in a snowstorm.

Published in the United States of America by
Rand McNally & Company, 1984
© 1983 Piero Dami Editore, Italy
All rights reserved
Printed in Italy G.E.P. - Cremona

ISBN 0-528-82562-3

Library of Congress Catalog Card No. 84-60933

The Woodland Folk Meet
The Gnomes

Tony Wolf

Rand McNally & Company

Chicago · New York · San Francisco

The Forest of the Gnomes

"Look! What's that over there?"
"Where?"
"Over there, on the bank of the stream."
"Oh, dear! It's a squirrel. Poor little thing! It's been drowned!"
"Quick! Let's run and see."
"Yes! Hurry!"
Who are these people? They are two gnomes, and now they rush to the stream where Squirrel is lying, white tummy upwards, soaked to the skin. The gnomes bend over him and one places a hand on Squirrel's heart.
"He's not drowned!" he exclaims, "He's still alive!"
"Quick! We must give him artificial respiration!"
The pair of gnomes start to revive Squirrel. One pumps his front legs up and down while the other massages his heart. They do this for some time, till Squirrel begins to gasp:
"Glurp! Glurp! Glurp!" and opens his eyes.
"Hurrah!" cheer the gnomes. "We've done it!"
"Glurp! Glurp! Glurp!"
"Is that all you have to say? What's your name? Where have you come from? How did you get into that mess?"
Squirrel shakes his head and sits up.
"Who am I?" he says. "I'd like to know who you are, with beards and red caps! Who are *you*?"
"We're gnomes," comes the reply, and one of them adds, "We live here, at the top end of the forest. Where do you come from? We've never seen you around here before."
"Oh, dear gnomes! Please be kind and help my friends!"
"Your friends? Where are they?"
Squirrel describes how all the woodland creatures set out to reach the top

"Stop! You're tickling me!"

"I wonder if the gnomes grow carrots!" says Rabbit to himself.

end of the forest in order to escape the terrible floods.

"They sent me on ahead," he continues, "to explore, but my boat capsized in a whirlpool, and if you hadn't come along . . . Brr! I shudder to think!"

"Don't worry! Let's go and look for your friends," says one of the gnomes.

"Yes," says the other, "and I'll fetch a boat and catch up with you."

A little later, Squirrel and the gnomes arrive under a huge fir tree which, until the previous day, had been half under water. Many of the woodland creatures' boats (boxes, nests and cartons), have been trapped in its branches. Now that the water has drained away, creatures and boats have been left high and dry.

"Come down!" call the gnomes. "Don't worry, you're safe now!"

"Who are you? Where are we?"

"We're gnomes, and you're in our country. Come on down!"

"Are they to be trusted?" murmur the Mouse Sisters.

"I think so," says Hedgehog.

Bright and bustling once again, Squirrel leaps into the tree and is now shouting:

"Come along! They're friendly! They saved my life!"

Reassured by this, the woodland folk begin to come out of the fir tree, sliding down ropes or sheets knotted together.

The Frogs prepare to dive. Suddenly one of the gnomes asks:

"I say! Whose hat is this?"

"It's Crow's!" exclaims Black Rat. "He must have drowned!"

"Crow! Crow! Where are you? Are you still alive?" they all shout.

There is no reply and Tortoise exclaims:

"I know! Crow has lost his hat and he's hiding so we can't see his bald head!"

At this, everyone starts laughing. The only person not laughing is Dormouse. He simply snores happily on.

"Anyway," he said to himself just as he dropped off to sleep, "I'm wearing a lifebelt."

Everyone comes down from the tree and trustingly shakes hands with the gnomes.

"Pile everything into our boat and climb on board," they say.

In the meantime, other boats with more gnomes sail up and soon all the woodland folk have been collected, safe and sound. And a little later, they are back on dry land, in their new country.

The Cart Race

Two months have passed. Spring is over and the floods are a distant memory. The woodland folk have become used to living at the top end of the forest, and they get on very well with the gnomes, who are great workers, industrious, clever, patient and, above all, very kind. Indeed, they're so kind, they've made . . .

But let's take things at an easy pace, just like the Tortoises! Poor Tortoises! Now that the weather is turning hot and it is nice to go for a dip in the stream, they can't keep pace with the others, so when they do reach the water, all hot and bothered, everyone else has finished drying himself and is ready to go back.

"Oh, dear! Shall we ever find a way to overcome our slowness?" asks a Tortoise sadly.

"Who knows!" says Bee. "We could ask the gnomes!"

"What can the gnomes do about it?"

"Oh, you never can tell!"

Which is very true. In fact, the gnomes feel sorry for the Tortoises and they decide to do something to help. They think and think and rack their brains, till an idea comes to them. One fine day, Clover, the carpenter gnome, calls the Tortoises and tells them:

"Stop looking so glum! From now on, you'll be as fleet of foot as the hare. In fact, even more so!"

"What! How can we ever be that?"

"Easy! Look at this!" and Clover shows them the carts, with their well-oiled four wheels, that he and his carpenter's mate have built.

"There! Try getting on! Don't be alarmed! Who wants to be first to try?"

"Whew! What a struggle! I'm exhausted." "But we've only just started," says Bee.

CARTS
MADE
HERE!
12

"I do!" exclaims one of the Tortoises (the slowest of them all).

"Good! Now get on to the cart. That's it! Now dig your feet into the ground and push yourself forward. Come on! Like that!"

"Yippee!" screeches Tortoise, and off he goes on the cart, quickly picking up speed and bowling along.

"Yippee! I'm flying!" he yells, whizzing round a corner and out of sight.

"OHHH!" gasp the other Tortoises in amazement, while the gnomes gaily ask:

"Well, what did we tell you?"

That is only the beginning of the construction of made-to-measure carts: racing carts, sedan carts and even some trucks too. All the woodland folk are dying to try the exciting experience of speed, even though, now and again, someone doesn't grip tightly enough and goes head over heels! What excitement there is in the forest! And what terrific fun for the Tortoises!

There are constant shouts of, "Out of the way! Out of the way!"

And if you don't jump smartly to one side, you run the risk of being run over by a Tortoise speeding along the path, with Bumblebee or Cricket in the passenger seat!

From this to real cart racing is just a short step. And to everyone's delight and general excitement, the Alphabet Grand Prix is held. The flag is lowered, the starter shouts, "They're off!" and the Tortoises, each with his racing number, are away at top speed around the track, screeching around corners, tearing uphill and juggling for position on the straight.

Who ever would have dreamed that Tortoises could flash past at such a rate? And they go so fast that, after the first crash and bump on the head, some of them think it would be a good idea to use a pumpkin as a crash helmet!

"Have you any idea how you're going to brake?" Bumblebee asks Number 10.

The Greatest Artist of Them All

There's such a great hustle and bustle along the forest pathways that the gnomes are planning to make some road signs to regulate the traffic. You always need to be careful, be constantly on the alert, not run anyone down and try not to get hurt. The other day, for example, one of the Tortoises did not manage to apply his brakes in time. He fell into a Mole hole and had to be taken to hospital!

Cornflower, the artist gnome, and his assistant are kept very busy. Frog too, who has been appointed traffic policeman, has his hands full.

"Do you understand," he asks a Tortoise about to try out a new type of scooter, "when you see this sign, it means there's a Snail crossing? Is that quite clear? When you see this other sign, you have to leave the roadway. Scooters are not allowed. Anybody found breaking the highway code will get a whopping fine!"

Other signs are being made to show, for example, where you must not pick the flowers or where poisonous toadstools grow, and folk are always being warned they mustn't light fires in the forest. A forest fire would be a dreadful disaster! But the artist gnomes paint other things too.

The Ladybirds are having the time of their lives playing hopscotch, hopping from one numbered square to the next without touching the lines.

Now they'd like a new game. That's why they go to the gnomes. Cornflower covers all the spots on their wing cases with red paint, then paints on black dots. The Ladybirds can now play dominoes!

And that's not all! He has even painted red spots on Frog's underwear!

It's Cornflower that does the artwork. He's the "Greatest Artist of them All." It's written in Latin on the beam over the studio door. He was the artist that painted that splendid portrait of old Owl and the famous picture of the White Bearded Ancient Gnome you see at the top of the page.

"Don't you get bored always playing the same game?"

Pictor optimus
Toad-
stools
Flowers
All the latest colors.
Model wings from Paris.
A
B
D
E
G
H
8

Being an artist, Cornflower would love to see the whole world full of colors. Which is why Weasel comes along one day, carrying a basket of eggs.

"Cornflower," he says, "I rob . . . er, I was lent . . . um, I got these eggs as a present from some bird friends of mine. I was going to make a meal of them, but folk say you're clever at decorating eggs, so here they are! If you'll paint them for me, I can keep them as ornaments or give them to my friends at Easter."

"All right," replies Cornflower, "I'll paint your eggs, in exchange for a spot of jam that I'm sure you'll easily manage to find . . . er . . . get as a present from some friend or other."

At that moment, several Moths go by and when Cornflower sees them, he groans, "Oh, no! No! That will never do!"

"What won't do?" ask the Moths.

"Your wings! So drab and gray! Why, folk wear their prettiest clothes to go out in the evenings, yet you go around looking like that!"

"What can we do about it?"

"Come here! A gnome friend of mine lives in a French forest. He's sent me some gorgeous butterfly wing models, the latest fashion, straight from Paris! Look at these!"

Cornflower shows them the gloriously colored wings.

"Oh, they're gorgeous!" gasp the Moths. "Could . . . could you paint our wings like these?"

"I could indeed! For a little honey, a nut or two and a packet of pine seeds!"

Shortly after, the Moths are proudly displaying their beautiful colored wings, while Paris fashions become all the rage amongst the beetles, crickets and all the other insects. Each tries his best to be the most elegant, original and colorful.

The world is ever so much more cheerful with a splash of color!

"I chose a black outfit with red spots. It makes me look slimmer!"

The Elevator

There are many beauty spots at the top end of the forest, and each woodland creature makes a new home there. The Mouse Sisters and all the former tenants of Oak Tree Terrace decide to stay neighbors. So they dig and scoop, saw and work at an old hollow tree and there build four very comfortable apartments. A wooden ladder leads from one floor to the next.

One unlucky day, Black Rat has a nasty accident as he is climbing the ladder to visit Hedgehog.

CRACK! One of the rungs suddenly gives way.

"AAH! My leg!"

Someone rushes to the rescue. Black Rat has really hurt himself. He has broken his leg! Beaver sets it in splints and then starts to make a pair of crutches. Just then, along comes Clover, the carpenter gnome.

"Yes, I see what's happened," says Clover. "Something must be done about that, for accidents are bound to happen when you have to go up and down ladders. Leave it to me!"

Two or three days later, Clover brings several gnomes to the apartments standing on a beautiful site close to a stream. They are carrying posts, planks, ropes, hammers and nails, pulleys and such like.

"What are you going to do?" asks Squirrel.

"Build an elevator," replies Clover.

"A what?"

"Don't you know what an elevator is?"

"No, I don't."

"Well, it carries people up and down. You'll soon see for yourself."

To the amazement of the woodland folk, the gnomes set to work and a few days later the elevator is ready for use. It's quite incredible! The car is built of red planks, has a stout rope and a heavy stone as a counterweight. It stops at every floor, so there's no need for a ladder.

"Now then," says Clover, "who's going to be first?"

"Did you see Black Rat's fall from the ladder?"

4
2
1

Now, if truth be told, the woodland folk are just a little afraid of it. Tortoise murmurs, "I'm not setting foot in that thing!"

"Craaw! Craaw! I say and repeat, Craaw! Neither am I!" croaks Crow. "I don't need an elevator anyway!"

"Black Rat broke a leg falling off a ladder," remarks Owl, "but you could break your neck in that thing!"

However, one of the Mouse Sisters steps bravely forward.

"Honestly! What cowards you all are! I'll ride in the elevator with Clover! Off we go! Third floor!"

Beaver, not to be outdone, then exclaims:

"I'll come too! Let's go!"

And so the trial run takes place amidst the general curiosity and excitement of all. The two Mouse Sisters left behind are worried, but Clover reassures them:

"Everything is going to be perfectly all right! Now, Beaver, lower the stone!"

The stone is gently lowered and the elevator equally gently begins to rise. The woodland folk stare in surprise. Never in all their lives have they seen such a thing before! And when the elevator reaches the third floor, they clap loudly.

Beaver is appointed Elevator Attendant. His job is to operate it and keep an eye on things. You need to be careful, of course. Too many passengers and the elevator would be overloaded. However, one after the other, everyone goes for a ride. In the end, even Owl comes to a decision:

"Hmmph!" he hoots. "I suppose I might as well try it too."

"Now, Water Rat, don't make the whole thing collapse, as usual!"

Hedgehog and the Apples

Hedgehog is a total glutton, and he specially loves apples. From time to time, he borrows a boat from the gnomes and off he goes, relying on his sense of smell and intuition. When he does return, the boat is always packed with delicious, sweet-smelling rosy apples.

The gnome who lends him the boat asks:

"What are you going to do with all these apples?"

"What a question! Eat them, of course! What do *you* do with apples?"

"Well, we eat some. But mostly we drink them."

Hedgehog stares at him in astonishment.

"Drink them! Are you teasing me?" he asks.

"Have you ever set eyes on such a lot of lovely apples?" Hedgehog asks.

"Not at all!"

"How can you drink an apple?"

The gnome smiles gently, then says, "Come with me and find out."

The gnome takes Hedgehog to a wonderful place where the apples are squeezed, grated and crushed. The sweet juice is then thoroughly mixed, before being poured into a series of barrels, from which it goes into small casks.

"The apple juice ferments and matures in the casks. Then when the time is ripe, we draw if off, and it's then called cider."

"What?"

"Cider! It's delicious, you know! Here!" The gnome takes some of the fragrant fizzy golden liquid from a cask. He fills two glasses, one for himself and the other for Hedgehog.

"Taste this!"

Hedgehog hesitates, then takes a sip.

"Mmm! This . . . this is very nice!" he exclaims.

"What did I tell you!"

"Now! I'm going to bring here all the apples from the boat and we'll turn them into cider. Hooray!"

A little later, with Frog's help, Hedgehog carries all his apples to the big hut, and when the gnomes find out a load of apples has come in, they rush along.

"Mmm," remarks Frog, peering into

a cask, "that's a pleasant smell! I would love to swim in there!"

In the meantime, Hedgehog has noticed a gnome busy at a lighted furnace, on top of which stands a strange copper object with a spiralling tube ending in an old barrel.

"What's that for?" he asks.

"For making apple brandy."

"Apple brandy! What's that?"

The gnome fills a glass and hands it to Hedgehog.

"Here, taste this!"

The first sip makes Hedgehog's eyes pop, the second sip makes him splutter, but after the third sip, he exclaims:

"Mmm! This is good! Isn't it strong! And it warms your tummy!"

"Of course it does! That's why we drink it in winter, when it is cold out of doors. We even have an expert brandy taster! Come along, I'll introduce you to him!"

The taster gnome is in a nearby cellar. He has a very important job, and very delicate too. He's the person who decides when the brandy has reached exactly the right stage of maturity, or if it is too strong or too mild, and so on. He wears a special cap and uses a special dish, called a tasting spoon. His nose is always bright red, of course, and would be even redder if the magician gnome did not treat it with a certain lotion that we'll be hearing about later.

"What a lot of glasses on that table," exclaims Hedgehog. "What are they for?"

"There's a special shape of glass for each kind of cider and brandy," the taster gnome explains.

"Well, I didn't know that before! What a lot I have learned, including the fact that you can drink apples! You've taught me so many things! Thank you."

"This is the very last taste, otherwise I'll never find the way home!"

The Miraculous Lotion

Crocus, the magician gnome, is working in his laboratory, when he hears a loud CRASH, THUMP in the next room. He dashes in to see what has happened, and finds his assistant, Coltsfoot, sitting on the floor below a shelf. Or rather, below an up-turned jar from which a thick yellow liquid is trickling over his bald head.

"Coltsfoot!" exclaims the magician gnome. "What has happened?"

"My goodness! I was just going to clasp that pot up there when my foot slipped. I fell, and on the way down, knocked over the jar, and as the jar fell, the stuff inside started to pour over my head!"

"So I see! That's the taster gnome's anti-red-nose lotion! Why don't you get up?"

"I feel such a fool. I don't feel I can get up!"

"Don't be silly! Come on, up you get and wash your head!"

Coltsfoot does as he is told.

However, only a few minutes later, the magician gnome hears a yell from the room next door.

"Now what is it!" he mutters angrily, as he dashes away to investigate. He stares dumbfounded. For Coltsfoot, who has always had a high forehead and receding hairline, is now sporting a thick mop of shiny locks, right down to his very eyebrows!

"Whh . . . whh . . . whh . . ." stutters Crocus. Coltsfoot exclaims:

"My hair has grown! The anti-red-nose lotion makes your hair grow! It's the discovery of the century!"

Some days later, the whole forest is buzzing with excitement. Word has spread that Coltsfoot has opened a shop and is selling a miraculous lotion for bald heads, at the price of three shells per dose.

"Yes, folks," he announces from the doorway, "it's guaranteed! Use a drop of this lotion and your hair will grow thick like mine!"

"What's happened this time?"

Just imagine the delight of those troubled by baldness! Along comes Black Rat. Only his sideburns are thick. Then Mole, who's losing his fur. Up comes Fox with a threadbare tail, and Crow too.

"Craaw! Craaw! I repeat, Craaw! At last, I can get rid of my bowler hat!"

Frog arrives, poking his nose into things as usual, and Hedgehog as well, who is all mixed up. He thinks Coltsfoot is selling a special kind of brandy! Then the magician gnome appears, feeling ever so embarrassed and with, as you can see, a shiny bald head. He waits his turn and says to himself:

"Just think! What a comedown! Having to buy my own lotion from my own assistant!"

However, in a matter of minutes, everyone has grown a thick fur coat or a mop of hair. And they are all absolutely thrilled. But . . . Yes, I'm afraid there's always a "but."

A couple of days later, Coltsfoot removes his cap to comb his hair, and to his horror, finds he has gone bald again!

"But . . . but what's happened?" he stammers. "My lovely hair. Where is it? Where has it gone? Does this mean . . ."

Yes, it does. It means that, the very next day, along come Black Rat, Mole, Fox and Crow.

"Just look!" they complain. "We're as bald as ever! Your lotion is quite useless!"

"Craaw! Craaw! I say and repeat, Craaw! We want our shells back!"

And so, with a heavy heart, Coltsfoot is obliged to refund them their shells and shut his shop. Yes, the anti-red-nose lotion *will* cause your hair to grow, but it also makes it all fall out a day or two later. What a pity!

A very quiet Coltsfoot returns to the magician gnome's laboratory, but the magician gnome simply remarks:

"Hmm! I'm afraid we'd better learn to live with our bald heads. Now, Coltsfoot, just take that book, and let's go back to work!"

"I'm getting hard of hearing. I'll have to do something about it," says the magician gnome.

A Trip in a Hot-Air Balloon

Guess who turns up in the forest one fine day, along with the migrating quails? Thumper the Fat Quail himself! That greedy quail, who was so tubby he couldn't get off the ground!

Just look at him now! He's been on a diet and is in splendid form!

"Oh, yes," he informs folk, "I can fly beautifully now. No more problems. If you knew the number of trips I've made! And the lands I've visited! You folks," he goes on, "never see anything."

"Well," Mole says, "we did travel from the foot of the wood to the top end."

"Ha! Ha! That *is* funny! What I mean

"The last time I was in Africa . . ."

are *real* trips, up in the sky! I'm talking about flying from Europe to Asia, then on to Africa! The foot of the wood to the top end, indeed! Ha! Ha! That's nothing!"

All the creatures are rather crestfallen at Thumper's scorn, and the gnomes too feel a little downhearted.

"We don't like traveling," the gnomes say. "We're used to our forest, we're not interested in visiting new lands." Then, turning to the woodland folk, they continue: "But if you'd like to travel . . ."

"Like to travel!" exclaims Frog.

"Well, you see, we can help you."

"But the point is, we want to fly, like the quails!"

"Oh, yes," agree the gnomes, "we can make you fly."

"FLY!!" The woodland folk stare in amazement. "But surely only birds, butterflies and other winged insects are able to fly?"

The gnomes smile a secret smile, then say:

"Leave it all to us!"

Several days later, the gnomes call all the woodland folk to come and see what they have built.

"It's a hot-air balloon!" they announce.

"What's a hot-air balloon?"

"Come with us and you'll soon see!"

A hot-air balloon is an enormous ball

which, when filled with hot air, floats up into the sky, rather like children's balloons. Underneath hangs a large basket known as the "car." Blown along by the wind, the hot-air balloon can travel from one land to another and across the seas.

The astounded woodland folk just stand and stare at it.

"You did say you'd like to fly," remark the gnomes. "Well, here's your craft! Who's going up in it?"

"I am!" chorus Shrew, Frog, Mole and Water Rat, and they scramble into the basket.

A mooring rope anchors the balloon to the ground. One of the gnomes, clutching a hatchet, calls out:

"Are you ready?"

"Yes!" shout back the ballooners.

"Steady! Go!" cries the gnome, cutting the rope. The balloon swiftly sails into the sky, while Blackbird, Butterfly and some of the other flying insects flutter round, waving.

"Hurrah!" shriek those left on the ground.

However, one or two mutter in worried tones, "They're quite mad!"

Mad? Nonsense! Flying is great fun! You can see the entire wood: there's the stream, the lake and the hills. There's the gnome's village, and farther away, the plains. Where will our ballooners travel? To Asia, or perhaps Africa?

Alas, they don't go very far. For barely half an hour later, they begin to hear a strange sound that goes SSSSSSSsssss.

Frog asks, "What's that noise?"

"It sounds like air hissing," replies Mole.

And that is exactly what it is. Air hissing from a tiny hole in the skin of the balloon, which starts to deflate and drop towards earth. Down, down, down it goes, while the earth rushes up to meet them.

"Help! We're going to crash!" they scream, as the hot-air balloon drops faster and faster, till . . . CRASH!

Their flight is over. Back to earth. Goodbye, Africa! Goodbye, Asia! But fortunately they are not hurt.

"Flying indeed! I'd far rather stay on the ground and go tunneling!" says Mole to himself.

The Golden Key

The magician gnome's attic is full of trunks, chests and boxes. They've lain there for centuries. Goodness knows who put them there! All are thick with dust.

Crocus, the magician gnome, patiently cleans and opens them, one by one. Inside one, he finds recipes, inside another, a big book, a history of the gnomes, while another reveals a list of all the grasses, flowers and mushrooms in the forest.

In the last . . . Alas, he can't see what's in the last one. It is locked. As he fiddles with the lock, he realizes that it is glinting like gold, and that the metalwork too is pure gold. But the key is nowhere to be seen.

"Craaw! Craaw! I say and repeat, Craaw! Does it matter if you haven't the key?" croaks Crow. "I'll open the trunk with a lever!"

"No! That's not allowed! We never use force, not even against objects. We'll all just have to search for the key."

At that moment, along comes one of the Mouse Sisters. She says:

"Oh, please run and call the doctor gnome. Otter is ill. He has a dreadfully high temperature!"

Otter is lying in bed, shivering feverishly. He went for a long swim in the pond and has caught a chill in the tummy. As he shivers, he stammers:

"Gold . . . all made of gold . . . down at the bottom . . . looks like . . . key."

The doctor gnome shakes his head worriedly.

"Dear me!" he murmurs. "Poor Otter is delirious! He says he has seen strange things!"

"Otter, what did you see?" asks Miss Mouse, trying to be helpful.

Sweating and shivering, Otter replies:

"Down there . . . but it's too deep . . . too dark . . . too cold . . ."

There is a moment's silence, then the magician gnome exclaims:

"At the bottom of the pond! That's where the key is!"

Everyone rallies round to lend a hand in retrieving the key. Dipper and Frog are asked to explore. They dive into the pond and, after searching and searching, finally manage to locate the key. But it is much too heavy for them to

"I hope they manage without my help."

bring to the surface. They are out of breath and it is so dark down there.

"We must find another way," say the gnomes. And after thinking things over, they decide to make a bathyscaphe (an underwater exploration vessel) and a submarine. With the help of the woodland folk, they set to work, and turn a pair of nice clean glass jars into a bathyscaphe and a submarine. One will be used to illuminate the bed of the pond, while the other will travel to the place where the key is lying, to supervise its retrieval.

Then they wait for a sunny day with no wind. The bathyscaphe disappears under the water and sinks slowly down through the water plants and curious fish, right down till it reaches the bottom, and the golden key is seen gleaming in the light of the lantern.

The explorer tugs the cord linking him to the gnomes on the surface to signal, "Key sighted! Send down the submarine and lower the hook!"

Soon after, the submarine slowly works its way down and a rope descends with a hook on the end of it. The whole operation is turning out to be very tricky and it's not going to be at all easy. By now, the fish are starting to look annoyed.

"We must hurry!" signals the gnome in the bathyscaphe. "The fish are glaring at us!"

It is Dipper who finally puts an end to the salvage operations, by fixing the key to the hook with his beak. He then darts back to the surface. He has no breath left and he feels his heart is ready to burst!

"Mission completed!" signals the bathyscaphe. "Returning to base! Hurrah!"

The golden key is presented with great ceremony to the magician gnome, and that very evening, all by himself, he opens the trunk. His hands are trembling. What will he find? An ancient book! The gnome slowly turns the pages and reads.

"OH!" he suddenly exclaims with a start, as though alarmed.

Alarmed? Why should he be alarmed?

Ah, well! We'll find that out in the next book, the book about the giants.

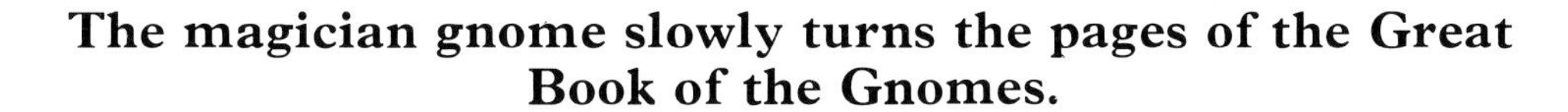

The magician gnome slowly turns the pages of the Great Book of the Gnomes.

The Forest Fire

Summer has come, and a scorching summer it is too. The last tiny cloud has gone from the sky, there's not a drop of rain in sight and the sun beats fiercely on the forest from dawn to dusk. Some of the springs have dried up, several ponds are bone dry and the Frogs that live there have had to search for a new home. The wind seems to have forgotten how to blow. The heat becomes more unbearable with each day that passes.

"A nasty state of affairs," comment the gnomes, "and dangerous!"

"Dangerous?" the woodland folk ask. "Why?"

"In this heat, a fire could break out any moment. All that needs to happen, far far away in the dry grass on the plains, is for . . . Well, what it means is that we must keep alert."

"How?"

"By taking turns to keep a lookout from the watchtower. The moment anyone notices something wrong, he rings the bell and raises the alarm."

They all begin to take turns. Each day a gnome and one of the woodland folk stand guard on the watchtower. Watch must be kept from dawn to dusk, from dusk to dawn. The only animal who doesn't stand guard is Dormouse. For obvious reasons!

It is night when Hamster, who is on duty, sees something like a shadow down in the forest, blotting out the stars where the sky and the forest seem to meet. He has another look, and what he sees makes his fur stand on end. Smoke! And . . . OH, NO! FIRE! The forest is alight!

"FIRE! FIRE! FIRE!" shrieks Hamster, tugging the bell with all his might.

Everyone leaps from bed, nest and den. "FIRE! The forest is alight! FIRE!"

The fire must be put out before it has time to destroy the entire forest.

"Spades! Saws! Axes! Collect all the tools! At once!"

"Who'll pull the fire engine?" someone asks.

"We'll take care of that!" say Badger and Wild Boar.

"Who'll carry the buckets?"

"FIRE! FIRE!"

"We will, on our scooters!" shout the Tortoises.

"Right! Let's be off!"

Thus begins the struggle against the forest fire. Fir trees are toppled to form a clearing, so that the other trees cannot catch fire. On the edge of the clearing, a trench is dug to check the flames, and water from the pond is dashed on to the burning grass. The full buckets are passed along a chain of gnomes, while the Tortoises go back with the empty buckets.

"Faster! Keep going! Faster!"

The fire engine races up and prepares to spray water on to the flames. Sparks are flying everywhere and one sets fire to the seat of a gnome's trousers. He flees, terrified.

"Wait till I put you out!" shouts one of his companions, rushing after him.

At that moment, the sound of wings is heard in the sky.

"Hooray! It's the fire-fighting squadron!"

Five large Mallard Ducks come into sight, each piloted by a gnome, and each carrying a big tin of water round its neck to drop on the fire. The brave Ducks skim low over the flames, then sheer off back to the pond for more water. It is a long, hard battle, fought in the flickering glow of the fire. But though it roars and crackles, the fire is unable to leap past the trench. And after a while, it starts to die down.

"Keep at it! We're winning!" they cry.

And all the gnomes and woodland folk redouble their efforts, till at last, the flames start to go out.

When morning dawns, the sun rises on a forest that is almost burnt away, and thick with smoke. But at least the flames have gone out. The gnomes and the woodland folk go home. They are tired, but happy and victorious.

And they all set off for home, tired and covered with grime, but well pleased with themselves!

The Theater in the Wood

Candytuft the gnome, Mouse and Ladybird are off to look for the first blueberries or some other early autumn fruit, when they hear "flop, flop, flop," followed by "whirr, whirr, whirr," and much chattering, chuckling, and flapping of wings.

What is going on? Who is making all the noise? They crouch down and, taking care to move quietly, they creep through the grass. And who should they see but Magpie, Dove and Heron, who is flapping his huge wings and saying:

"You see? That's what they do. And the folk at the theater clap their hands! I can tell you, it's really lovely!"

"I'm sure you're right," Magpie agrees, "but folk here haven't the slightest interest in plays!"

"There isn't even a theater here," adds Dove.

"That's just what I was saying!" Heron continues. "The theater I saw was a long way away from here!"

And so saying, the three birds spread their wings and fly away.

"These birds are quite mad," mutters Mouse. "What good is a theater?"

"Nevertheless," says Candytuft, "I think they're right. A theater is important, and it's exactly what we need. But let's see what we can do about it. Let's go home and forget about the blueberries. I've got an idea."

To begin with, Candytuft's idea leaves everyone speechless, but then they all start to feel enthusiastic. Gnomes and woodland folk all set to work. Some saw the wood, others hammer in nails, others do the decorating, some make costumes, some write, others read, and there are those who are learning things off by heart.

But what are the woodland folk busily making? That question is easily

"As for myself, I'm an actor," says Heron.

Romeo
and
Juliet

answered: a theater. And they're putting on a play!

A few weeks later, Wild Boar pulls a rope and opens the curtains at the Forest Theater. The orchestra strikes up and the audience, which has paid 3 shells each for a ticket, is applauding wildly. Absolutely everyone is there, not one person is missing. Mouse, who doesn't have any shells for a ticket, is perched on stilts, and Crow has stuck his head through the bamboo fence in order to see.

The play begins. Owl is the prompter, Cornflower takes the part of the Good King, Fox is the Wicked Queen, Frog and one of the Mouse Sisters are the romantic couple, Romeo and Juliet.

It is a heart-wrenching tale that makes you sigh and shed tears. Princess Juliet wants to marry Romeo the poet. The King agrees to the marriage, but the Queen has no intention of letting her daughter wed a penniless poet, so the young couple run away, but they are caught by the palace guards (played by the Tortoises). The Princess is condemned to imprisonment in a tower and Romeo is to be beheaded.

However, just as Romeo is about to be handed over to the soldiers, Juliet appears, having escaped from prison. On their knees, the young couple beg for their lives, and are pardoned. Amidst tears and applause, it all ends happily with a wedding.

"That was lovely!" says Heron. "It really was a very good play!"

"We thoroughly enjoyed it!" agree Magpie and Dove.

And all the gnomes and woodland folk go contentedly off to bed. Nobody could remember spending such an enjoyable evening!

However, a play like that calls for a lot of time and hard work. The theater itself has to be built. And what if it rains on the night of the performance?

Then Clover the carpenter gnome had a brilliant idea. Puppets! Woodland folk puppets, of course! Miss Mouse, Badger, the gnomes, the Frogs, everyone!

Now, performances can be held in all weathers, and in winter too, even if it's snowing.

"Now, let me see, where does this go?"

An SOS in the Snow

Yes indeed, winter! It's on its way, there is no doubt about that. The sky is laden with gray clouds and a bitterly cold wind is blowing.

Some of the gnomes say:

"Hmm. It could snow any time now."

But the gnomes' juniper berry picking squad wants to set out just the same.

"Be careful! It's cold. It might start to snow!"

"No, it won't," says Catmint, the leader. "I'm sure it won't. My right foot hurts when there's snow on the way, and today I don't feel the slightest twinge."

"Take care! The juniper patch is a long distance away."

"Don't worry, we've plenty of food."

So the four gnomes set off. They travel deeper and deeper into the forest for several days, till one evening they reach the place where the juniper bushes grow.

"Let's build a hut," they say, "and start picking tomorrow."

Tired and sleepy, the gnomes go to sleep in the hut. During the night, however, Catmint wakens with a ghastly pain in his foot. He peers out anxiously.

Oh, dear! Everything is white! Snow is gently drifting from the sky and is already several inches deep on the ground.

"How are we going to get home now?" the gnomes wonder next morning, when they look out and see the whole forest white with snow.

"All the paths are buried! What can we do?"

"My foot's hurting! That's a bad sign! It's going to snow," says Catmint.

"We are in a fix! There isn't much food."

"Well, don't let's start worrying now. Let's pick the juniper berries. Then we can decide what to do!"

The gnomes begin to pick the berries, but Catmint's foot is painful and it starts to snow again, so heavily that the forest seems to be lying under a great white mantle.

Two days pass and, alas, the food is almost gone. The gnomes' anxiety is now turning into real alarm.

"Keep calm! The others will come and look for us," says Catmint reassuringly.

"Yes, but how will they find us? How will they know where to look?"

"Listen! I hear wings! And coming this way! Hurray!"

Indeed a sound of wings is coming from above. The gnomes rush outside and they see Peregrine Falcon searching for them. He is too high up, and passes overhead without noticing the gnomes or hearing their shouts.

"Ahoy! Peregrine! Here! Come back! We're here!"

All their shouting is in vain. Peregrine flies farther and farther away from them. The gnomes are downcast now, but Catmint does not lose hope.

"I know!" he exclaims. "I have an idea! Holly berries!"

"Holly berries?"

"Yes, red ones! There are heaps of them! Come on!"

As they go, Catmint explains what he has in mind, and there, a few hours later, across the snow sprawl the letters SOS, marked in red holly berries. And it is not long before help arrives. As he wheels over the forest again next day, Peregrine sees the SOS and flaps down. He has a pilot gnome on board.

"It's all right, now I've found you," cries the pilot gnome to his friends on the ground, waving their arms. "It's all right! We'll rescue you without delay!" And wheeling away, he speeds back to the village.

An hour or two later, a sleigh drawn by the two Fawns, sets out loaded with food: honey, walnuts, black bread, and a generous amount of apple brandy, all provided by the Green Shamrock, the gnomes' Emergency and Protection Service.

A sleigh, drawn by the Fawns, and loaded with food, sets off to meet the gnomes.

The Sick Doctor

On stormy days or moonlit nights when the snow sparkles, all is wrapped in silence and everyone is sound asleep, the gnomes in their houses and the woodland folk in dens and nests. But someone wearing snowshoes, with a scarf wound around his neck, walks through the wood, carrying a little black bag. Who is he? Can't you guess? It's Celandine, the doctor gnome. He's the gnome who comes each time he is called and treats every kind of illness, from upset tummies to the flu, from toothache to bronchitis. What would life in the forest be like without the doctor gnome?

Then one day, a strange thing happens. Celandine is called out, but does not appear. The patient waits and waits but no one comes. The doctor is probably only late. However, hours pass and no doctor gnome arrives. Surely he can't have forgotten? Impossible! Has he been discouraged by the cold and the snow? But that's impossible too! What then?

Someone runs to the doctor's house and knocks on the door. Nobody answers. So he goes inside. No sign of the doctor! The alarm is raised without delay and just as everyone is getting ready to form a search party, Mouse arrives with an incredible piece of news.

"The doctor is sick! Come quickly! He's at my house!"

The doctor sick! Goodness me! And who is going to treat *him*?

Hedgehog, Mole, Squirrel, Shrew, one of the Mouse Sisters and Water Rat all rush over to Mouse's house.

"In here," says Mouse, "in the bed-room."

And there lies the doctor, with a high temperature.

"Oh, oh," he moans under his breath. "Oh, dear, what a pain!"

"We must do something," urges Ladybird, arriving late and opening the doctor's bag.

Everyone crowds around. They take

"You've got a nasty attack of toothache."

his temperature, put a hot-water bottle on his stomach, look down his throat, and listen to his heartbeat.

"What's wrong with him?" asks Miss Mouse.

"I say it's chronic laryngitis," declares Mole.

"I'd say gastritis with complications," says Squirrel.

"I'd give him a penicillin injection," adds Hedgehog.

"I'd apply iodine," adds Mole.

"I'd operate on his stomach," says Squirrel.

At these words, Celandine opens his eyes in alarm and murmurs:

"No, don't do a thing. Leave me where I am. I'll get better by myself."

"Impossible!" declares Hedgehog.

"Nobody gets better by himself," says Mole.

"It's against the Laws of Medicine!" adds Squirrel.

"Listen to me!" replies Celandine. "Do nothing at all! Just light the stove, fetch a bottle of apple brandy and give me a tablespoon every quarter of an hour."

The woodland folk do as they're told. Miss Mouse will be nursc and give Celandine, who has caught a nasty chill after all that trailing about in the snow, his doses of medicine.

But would you believe it! After the first tablespoonful of apple brandy, he is feeling better already!

Luckily, all is well. However, you can't do without a doctor can you? So Black Rat takes on the task of treating the patients. He puts on a fine white coat and opens an office with a notice which says:

"Dr. Black Rat, General Medicine, temporary substitute for Dr. Celandine. Office hours: 10-12, 3-6. All kinds of treatment for every sort of illness. Complete cure guaranteed."

And do you know, Black Rat really does cure every patient! All kinds of treatment for every sort of illness. But the treatment never varies. No matter what is wrong with the patient, whether he really is ill or just imagines he is, Black Rat doles out the same medicine for sore throats, broken legs and stiff necks: a large spoonful of castor oil!

One or two patients get better without any treatment at all. Beaver, for example, takes one look and says to himself, "What a clever doctor! The sight of him makes me feel better already!" And off he goes!

"I think I'll just suffer my toothache rather than swallow that castor oil," says Beaver to himself.

The Great Monument

It was Hare's idea. And he was sure it was a jolly good idea. He told Fox about it, who told Tortoise, who spoke to Beaver, who spoke to Hamster, who told Bear, who told the Mouse Sisters. In other words, all the creatures came to hear about it, and they held a meeting to come to a decision. The only one left in the dark is Hedgehog. When he sees everyone in a huddle, talking away in low voices, he asks:

"What's going on?"

"I'll tell you," says Squirrel. "Listen to this. Winter's almost over and a whole year has passed. It'll soon be the first anniversary of our arrival at the top end of the forest. And we like it here, don't we?"

"Of course we do!"

"Thanks to the gnomes, who've been so helpful, isn't that so?"

"It is!"

"In that case, we must thank them, mustn't we?"

"We certainly must!"

"So we've decided to erect a monument, as a thank you present."

"A monument? To whom?"

Squirrel shakes his head patiently.

"To the gnomes, of course!"

A Gnome Monument! What a splendid idea! Everyone is certain that the gnomes will be thrilled. So a Committee is elected and Beaver draws up the plans. They'll select one of the big sturdy forest trees – an oak or a fir – and carve a gnome on the trunk. Yes, a large gnome, complete with beard, moustache and cap, leaning on a fine mushroom, and standing on a beautifully decorated pedestal. Everyone is to lend a hand, and the Woodpeckers will

"We'll tell you all about it later. Don't prick us as usual!"

make the finishing touches with their sharp beaks before the painters start. For what kind of a Gnome Monument would it be without a coat of paint?

And so, each day, with one excuse or another, the woodland folk steal away to a secret corner of the forest and work busily at carving the monument.

However, all the coming and going arouses the gnomes' suspicions and, one day, unseen they silently creep along to the place where the woodland folk are hard at work. And such a surprise do they get that they cannot help exclaiming:

"Oh! Isn't that wonderful!"

To tell the truth, they arrive in the middle of great confusion. Beaver and Woodpecker are applying the finishing touches. The painters have just started work. Poor Squirrel who is sweeping up the shavings, gets blue paint on his head. Just then, one of the Mouse Sisters appears with a picnic basket. And everyone has a good feast.

"You've been ever so clever!" say the gnomes admiringly and quite overcome. "And so nice!"

"*You* have been clever and nice," reply the woodland folk, "and this monument will stand for hundreds of years, as a reminder of your kindness and goodness!"

Well, everyone is delighted. They hug each other and clap their hands. Dormouse, who is still hibernating and thinks it is night, pops his head out of his hole and sleepily asks:

"What's all the noise about? Can't a fellow sleep in peace?"

A few days later, everyone is even more delighted and excited when the monument is unveiled. What a day that is! The band marches along every path in the forest, playing the Pancake Song, and led by Marmot who thinks to himself:

"I wish Hedgehog would stop blowing his trumpet in my ear!"

While Hedgehog thinks to himself, "I wish Ladybird would stop whistling in my ear!"

And Mole thinks to himself, "I wish Ladybird would get out of my tuba!"

And Hamster thinks to himself, "I wish Beaver would stop banging me on the head!"

And Beaver thinks to himself, "I wish Water Rat would stop treading on my tail!"

At any rate, the band gaily plays our friends right out of this book. But it's accompanying them towards another book of further and even more exciting adventures.

And they all set off through the forest while the band played the Pancake Song.

Titles in this series

Meet the Woodland Folk

The Woodland Folk Meet the Gnomes

The Woodland Folk Meet the Giants

The Woodland Folk in Fairyland

The Woodland Folk Meet the Elves

The Woodland Folk in Dragonland